Robin Hood All At Sea

by

Jan Mark

Illustrated by Tony Ross

You do not need to read this page – just get on with the book!

First published in 2005 in Great Britain by
Barrington Stoke Ltd
18 Walker St, Edinburgh, EH3 7LP

www.barringtonstoke.co.uk

Reprinted 2007, 2009

ISBN: 978-1-84299-332-3

Printed in Great Britain by Bell & Bain Ltd

Meet The Author – Jan Mark

What is your favourite animal?
The noble rat
What is your favourite boy's name?
George
What is your favourite girl's name?
Marjorie
What is your favourite food?
Pickled herring
What is your favourite music?
Klezmer
What is your favourite hobby?
Listening to music

Meet The Illustrator – Tony Ross

What is your favourite animal?
A cat
What is your favourite boy's name?
Bill
What is your favourite girl's name?
Roxanne
What is your favourite food?
Lobster
What is your favourite music?
Irish
What is your favourite hobby?
Sailing

Contents

Chapter 1
In the Greenwood

The world is an unfair place. The rich get richer. The poor get poorer. Many people *think* this. But Robin Hood *did* something about it.

He stole money from the rich and gave it to the poor. That was fair but it was against the law and rich people made the laws. Poor people called Robin Hood a hero.

Rich people called him a robber and an outlaw.

When things got too hot for Robin, he had to hide. He lived in the forest with his friends and they went on robbing the rich and giving to the poor. Now they were all outlaws.

They called the forest the Greenwood. It was a fine place to live, but sometimes it was a little too green ...

In summer the trees were green. The grass was green, the weeds were green. Even the pond was green.

Robin Hood sat on a tree stump. "I'm sick of this," he said.

His best mate, Little John, walked by. His real name was John Little and he was very big. That was why he was called Little John. It was the outlaws' idea of a joke.

"What's up with you?" said Little John.

"I'm sick of green," said Robin Hood. "Look around you, everything's green."

"Of course it is," Little John said, "that's why we call it the Greenwood."

"Well, it's too green for me," Robin said crossly. "The trees are green, the grass is green, the weeds are green. Even I'm green."

"You should wash more often," Little John said. Robin jumped up and hit him. Little John hit Robin. They rolled around punching each other and fell in the pond. This happened quite often. The other outlaws stood around and watched them climb out. They stood there dripping. There was slime all over them.

"Now who's green?" Robin Hood said.

"Fighting again?" Maid Marian said. "Grow up."

Maid Marian was Robin's lady friend. She was never afraid to tell him what she thought. One thing she thought was that Robin should marry her. This made Robin nervous.

"He said I needed a wash," Robin said.

"Well, now you've had one," Little John snapped back. "What are you moaning about? *You* said you were green, I didn't."

"I meant my clothes," Robin yelled. "Green!"

"We all wear green," Will Scarlet said. "So we can't be seen in the Greenwood. It's called camouflage."

"I know that," Robin said. "It was my idea in the first place. But I've had enough of green. I can't stand it."

"Some people don't know when they're well off," Friar Tuck said.

"We're outlaws. We do as we please, we eat plenty, we drink well. We don't pay tax. We rob the rich and give the money to the poor."

"I'm sick of that too," Robin said.

"But we have to do it," Little John said. "We're outlaws." He thought about it. "I suppose we could rob the rich and keep the money."

"I've had enough," Robin said. "All these people we rob – they've got more money than us."

"Yes," Marian said, "they're the rich. That's why we rob them."

"There must be easier ways to earn a living," Robin said. "Look at the Sheriff of Nottingham. He's got more money than us."

"Not any more," Little John said. "We've stolen most of it."

"What about the Bishop?" Robin said.

"No. We cleaned him out last year," said Little John.

"The Earl?"

"No."

"Wait a bit," Friar Tuck said. "That sea captain we robbed last week. He had loads of cash."

"Not any more," Will Scarlet said. "We've got it."

"He had a fishing boat, didn't he?" Marian said.

"That's it!" Robin cried. "I'll go to sea. I'll be a fisherman. I'll leave the Greenwood."

"Don't be daft," said Little John. "What do you know about fishing?"

"I often go fishing."

"Yes, in the pond," Little John said. "The sea's a bit bigger than our pond."

"Don't try to talk me out of it," Robin said. "I've made up my mind."

"You'll need a boat."

"I'm not listening," Robin said. He started to hum loudly.

"Grow up," said Maid Marian.

"You'll be seasick."

"I'm already sick," Robin said. "Didn't I tell you? I'm sick of green. The sea is blue." He sang, "Hello, blue sea! Hello, blue sky!"

"Sometimes the sea is green," Little John told him.

Robin hit him. John hit him back. They rolled around punching each other and fell into the pond.

"Here we go again," said Marian.

Chapter 2
To the Blue Sea

Next morning Robin got ready to leave. He packed all his clothes into a sack and picked up his trusty longbow. He put it over his shoulder.

"You won't catch fish with a bow," Little John said. "Or are you going to hit them over the head with it?"

Robin took no notice of him. He picked up his quiver of arrows.

"What are you going to do, shoot the fish?" Friar Tuck said. "They don't stand still, you know."

Robin hummed loudly. "I'm not listening," he said.

"Grow up," said Maid Marian.

The outlaws went a little way with Robin to see him off. They stood and waved as he walked away through the trees. He waved back, but he did not turn round.

They could hear him singing.

"Hey-diddly-dee, a sailor's life for me!"

"I give him a week," Little John said.

"It'll take him a week to get there," Will Scarlet said.

"All right," Little John said, "two weeks."

"Two weeks and a day, then," Will said. "One week to get there, one week to come back, and one day in the middle, fishing."

"One day in the middle *not* catching fish," Little John said.

Friar Tuck wrote it all down and the outlaws all made bets. Marian bet that Robin would be back by tomorrow night.

Then they sat around wondering what to do. They were used to Robin giving the orders. In the end they went out and robbed the Sheriff of Nottingham, just to pass the time.

Meanwhile, Robin walked on and on across fields and farms. He had left the forest far behind him. But everything was still too green.

It took him six days to reach the sea. The outlaws had been wrong about that. At night he slept in barns and sheds. He knocked on the doors of farmhouses and cottages and asked for something to eat.

People said, "Who are you?"

"Robin Hood," said Robin.

The people didn't always believe him but they gave him something to eat anyway, just in case.

But some of them wanted proof.

"Where are your outlaws then?" they said.

"Oh, I left them at home," Robin said.

"You aren't going to rob me, are you?" said one old woman.

"Madam, I rob the rich and give to the poor," Robin told her. "I never rob poor people."

"Who are you calling poor?" the old woman shouted. "Cheek!" She threw a turnip at him.

"People around here don't understand me," Robin said to himself. He ate the turnip.

One morning he walked across a field and when he came to the other side there were no more fields to cross. He was on top of a cliff. The sea lay below him. It was blue.

"At last!" Robin shouted. "No more green!"

He stood on the edge of the cliff. The sea was a long way down. The beach was a long way down. At the end of the beach was a little town and there were some boats on the sand. Fishing boats.

"Hey-diddly-dee!" Robin sang. He started to walk down the cliff path and sniffed the salt sea air. The fresh wind blew through his hair.

He skipped along the beach. The sand got into his shoes but he didn't care. The sand was yellow, the cliff was white, the sea was blue. There was nothing green anywhere.

"I'm in heaven!" he cried.

A man walked past him along the beach.

"No, mate," he said. "That's the North Sea over there. And it's nothing like heaven, believe me."

"Are you a fisherman?" Robin said.

"Do I look stupid?" the man said, and went on stomping along the beach.

On the way into the town Robin passed the church. While he was walking through the churchyard he looked at the gravestones.

They had writing on them. They said things like

HERE LIES JAMES THE BAKER

HERE LIES MARY THE COOK

UNDER THIS STONE LIES
HENRY THE CARPENTER

There were no fishermen's graves. Robin wondered why.

Someone else was walking through the churchyard. It was the man Robin had met on the beach.

"You still here?" the man said.

"Where are the fishermen's graves?" Robin asked. "Don't fishermen die in this town?"

The man looked at him. "No, they don't," he said. "They die at sea. Their bodies are out there, under the waves."

Chapter 3
In the Dark Night

Robin left the churchyard very fast and walked on into the town. It didn't look like a place with much money in it.

He went down to the beach to see the fishing boats.

The fishermen didn't seem friendly.

"What are you hanging about for?" one of them said.

"Do you need any help?" Robin said. "I'm strong and willing."

"What can you do?" said the fisherman.

Robin thought about what he could do. He could shoot an arrow at a target and hit the bullseye, every time. He could chase deer and catch them. He could hunt rabbits. He was brilliant at robbing the Sheriff of Nottingham.

"I can do anything," he said.

"Can you join two ropes in a splice?" the fisherman asked.

"Er – no," said Robin.

"Can you raise a sail?"

"No."

"Then you're no good to me," the fisherman said.

It was the same at the next boat, and the next. The fishermen asked him if he could do things he had never heard of. No-one wanted to give him a job.

The sea was very rough now, the sky was dark and night was falling. Robin was tired of sleeping in barns and sheds. There were no barns in this town. All the sheds smelled of fish. He wished he was back in the Greenwood.

It doesn't look so green in the dark, he thought.

Just then a woman came down the lane. She was carrying a heavy basket on one arm and a baby on the other. Three little children walked behind her.

Robin Hood was a gentleman even if he was an outlaw. He knew how to behave.

"May I carry your basket, madam?" he said.

"It's very kind of you to offer, but I live just here," the woman said. "Perhaps you could open the gate for me?"

Robin opened the garden gate.

"You're a stranger in town, aren't you?" the woman said. "I haven't seen you before."

"I came here to find work," Robin said. "But I haven't had much luck so far. Now I'm looking for somewhere to sleep."

"I can rent you a room," the woman said, "and I may be able to give you a job. Come on in."

Robin opened the door for the woman and they all went into the house.

"What sort of work do you do?" the woman asked.

"I'm a fisherman," Robin said. He thought, *She's a woman. She won't know much about fishing.*

"You're the very man I'm looking for," the woman said. "My husband was a fisherman. He died last year and now I'm a widow, but I still have his boat. I rent it to some other fishermen. You look fit and strong. I'll tell them to give you work. Now, come and sit by the fire. We'll have supper when the children are in bed."

Robin and the fisherman's widow sat by the fire and talked. She asked him what his name was. He decided not to tell her in case she had heard about him. She might not want to have an outlaw in her house and on her boat.

"My name is Simon Wise," he said. "My friends call me Honest Simon."

This was a lie. In fact, it was two lies. Still, if you're an outlaw, you don't always tell the truth.

"Well, Simon, I like the look of you," the widow said. "Can you join two ropes with a splice?"

"I can," said Robin.

That was three lies.

"Can you raise a sail?"

"I can."

Four lies.

"Can you bait a hook and catch fish?"

"I can."

Well, that was true. He'd caught many fish in the green pond back in the Greenwood.

"Then you can sleep in my spare room tonight," the widow said. "Tomorrow we'll go and look at my boat. The skipper's in charge. I'll tell him to give you a job."

Robin went to bed and thought about his lies. He had never spliced a rope. He knew what a rope was but he had no idea how to splice one. He had never raised a sail. He had never been in a boat at all. The green pond in the Greenwood was the only water he knew.

Tomorrow he was going to sail on the rough North Sea. He thought of the grey

waves and the grey sky. He thought about
the man he'd met in the churchyard. He
thought about what the man had said.

"Fishermen die at sea."

Chapter 4
Under Grey Clouds

After breakfast the widow took Robin down to the beach to see her boat. She picked up the baby and the three little children ran behind her. Robin picked up his bow and arrows, out of habit.

"What are those?" the children said.

"Where I come from, we use them to catch fish," Robin told them. That was another lie.

The wind was blowing and the sea was still rough but the sun shone on the waves. The water seemed to be full of sparks.

"This is the boat," the widow said.

Robin had seen the boat before.

"And this is the skipper," the widow said.

Robin had seen the skipper before and the skipper had not forgotten him.

"This is Simon Wise," the widow said. "His friends call him Honest Simon."

The skipper looked at Robin, up and down.

"I want you to give him a job," the widow said. "He can splice a rope and raise a sail and bait a hook as well as any of you."

"Really?" the skipper said. "You could have fooled me." He glared at Robin. "You must have learned a lot since yesterday."

"Now, do it to please me," the widow said. "You know you need another man."

"Whatever you say," the skipper said, but he did not look happy.

"Good luck," the widow said, and went back along the beach to her house with the children.

"Now, what tales have you been telling her?" the skipper said.

"Let me work on your boat," Robin said. "You won't regret it."

"I'm regretting it already," the skipper said. He watched Robin climb into the boat. "Do you know what a landlubber is?"

"No," Robin said. His leg got tangled up with the longbow and he fell flat on the deck.

"A landlubber," said the skipper, "is a silly great lump who knows nothing about boats. And put that bow out of the way where you can't trip over it."

"What happened to that woman's husband?" Robin asked.

"He went over the side," the skipper said. "It was a windy day, like this. And a rough sea, like this."

Robin thought of the churchyard where there were no fishermen's graves. He thought about the man he had met. He thought about what the man had said.

"Fishermen die at sea."

The rest of the crew had begun to laugh when they saw Robin fall into the boat. And they went on laughing.

The men pulled up the anchor and raised the sail. With the wind behind it the boat rocked and rolled through the waves. They left the land far behind. The beach vanished, the town vanished. Last of all, even the cliffs vanished. There was nothing all around them but grey sea and grey skies.

The men baited their hooks with wriggling worms and leaned over the side of the boat. Robin baited his hook with a wriggling worm and leaned over the side. The wind blew, the waves swelled up and down, the boat rocked and rolled. The men caught fish. Robin was sick.

This went on all morning. By noon a heap of fish lay all shiny on the deck. Robin also lay on the deck. He was greener than he had ever been back in the Greenwood.

The skipper stepped over him. He did not look at Robin but he spoke loudly.

"On this boat," he said, "we share everything. We share our food, we share our drink and we share our fish. But we only share our fish," he went on, "if we catch any fish to share."

"Give me time," Robin said with a groan. "I'm not used to this boat yet. It goes up and down."

"You'd better get used to it," the skipper said. "All boats go up and down."

The crew laughed and baited their hooks again. Robin hadn't caught a fish yet so his hook still had the same old worm on it. He dangled it over the side. The worm had stopped wriggling. Fish looked at it and turned away.

The outlaws were right, he thought. *What am I doing? These fishermen think I'm a fool, and I am a fool. I just wish I could take them all home to the Greenwood. Then they'd see what kind of a man Robin Hood is. They'd see him when he's shooting arrows and chasing deer and fighting Little John and robbing the Sheriff of Nottingham.*

But, of course, the fishermen didn't know that he was Robin Hood. They thought he was Simon Wise, Honest Simon.

When they called him Simon he forgot to answer. He was too busy being sick. That made them laugh all the harder.

"Doesn't even know his own name," they said.

"Simon Wise? Honest Simon? Simple Simon, more like," said the skipper.

Then a shout went up.

"A sail! A sail!"

A dark shape was coming towards them. Another shout went up.

"It's a Frenchman!"

The dark shape came closer, moving very fast.

"Pirates!"

Chapter 5
The Black Sail

The pirate ship was nasty-looking and it had a black sail. Nasty-looking men stood on the deck. The sun shone on their swords.

"We're all lost," the skipper said. "They'll take our fish, they'll take our boat. They'll take us back to France in chains and throw us into prison."

"Well, what are you going to do about it?" Robin said. He sat up. Now he did not feel so sick.

"Do about it?" the skipper shouted. "What can we do about it? Look at those pirates. They've got knives and swords. Their ship is ten times faster than our boat. They'll run us down, and jump aboard. What can we fight them with? Fish hooks? Worms?"

Robin sprang up. He did not feel sick at all. He picked up his bow and grabbed an arrow.

"Don't be afraid," he cried. "Let them come closer and then we'll see who's master."

"Put that down," the skipper said, "and shut up. You'll have someone's eye out.

We've all had enough of your boasting and bragging, you useless great landlubber."

Robin raised his bow and let the arrow fly. But just at that moment, a great wave struck the boat and the arrow went straight up in the air. Everyone forgot about the pirates and stood watching it.

After a little while it came straight down again and hit the deck, not far from where the skipper was standing.

"Whose side are you on?" the skipper yelled. The arrowhead was stuck in the deck. The shaft was twanging gently.

Robin swore, under his breath. He tugged the arrow from the deck and grabbed a rope that was lying near it. Then he tied himself to the mast.

"We should have thought of that," the skipper said. "We'd have saved ourselves a lot of bother."

But now Robin could stay on his feet and keep his balance no matter how much the boat rocked and rolled. The other ship was very close now. The fishermen could see the pirates, armed to the teeth. They could even see those teeth, gleaming white in black beards.

Robin bent his bow again and let fly with another arrow. This one flew straight and true across the water and found its target in a pirate's heart.

The pirate gave a cry, threw up his arms and vanished. The other pirates growled and waved their swords, but the swords were useless and they knew it. Twenty pirates with knives and swords did not stand a chance against one man with a longbow.

The fishermen cheered.

"Bet you can't do that twice," the skipper said.

Robin shot another arrow and a second pirate fell dead. Then another and another.

One by one the pirates fell dead. And hung over the side of their ship like dirty washing.

At last only the captain was left. He waved his sword and flashed his teeth.

"You'll never take me alive!" he cried.

"We don't want to take you alive," Robin said, and shot his last arrow. It zipped from the bow, hissed across the water and hit the pirate captain with a dull thud.

The fishermen cheered again and waved their hats in the air. The skipper shook Robin by the hand.

"I knew you were a brave fighter as soon as I saw you," he said.

"You could have fooled me," said Robin.

By now the pirate ship was drifting close to the fishing boat.

"Change course!" the skipper yelled. "We don't want it ramming into us. Head for land. Our boat is safe. Our fish are safe, thanks to Simon."

"Hooray for Honest Simon!" the fishermen cheered. "Simon shall share our fish."

This time Robin Hood didn't forget that he was Simon Wise. He bowed and turned to the skipper with a modest smile.

"Never mind the fish," he said. "What about the ship? You're not just going to leave it drifting, are you?"

"Well, I suppose we could tow it home," the skipper said. "Maybe we can sell it."

"Listen," Robin said, "what kind of a ship is it?"

"It's a pirate ship," the fishermen said.

"And what do pirates do?" Robin asked them.

The fishermen growled. "They steal from honest men like us."

"So what will they have on their ship?"

The fishermen looked at each other.

"Fish!"

"No," Robin said, "I don't think so. They also steal from rich sea captains. I've done it myself," he added. "Let's get on board the ship and see what we can find. Follow me, boys!" he shouted. "This is what I'm good at."

Chapter 6
The Golden Prize

As soon as the pirate ship came close enough Robin jumped aboard. The fishermen followed.

First they threw the dead pirates into the sea. They were getting in the way.

Robin pulled out his trusty dagger and went down into the cabin. He wanted to be sure that there were no pirates still lurking about. Then he led the way into the hold. This was a dark place in the bottom of the ship where the pirates kept their treasure.

"Bring a light!" he shouted. The skipper came in with a lantern. The fishermen crowded in behind them and they stood there with their mouths open.

There were oak sea chests all around them, with huge iron locks. Heavy sacks lay in the corners of the hold. They clinked when people kicked them.

"Bring it all up on deck," Robin said. "Then we'll be able to see what we're doing."

The fishermen carried the sacks and chests up to the deck. Robin slit open the sacks with his dagger. The skipper found an axe and chopped the lids off the chests.

The sacks were filled with jewels. Brooches and buckles, earrings and necklaces and bracelets poured onto the deck. There was even a crown in one of the sacks.

"These were high-class pirates," the skipper said.

The chests were filled with coins.

Everyone sat around staring. They had never seen so much money in all their lives.

"What shall we do with it all?" one of them said.

"I'll tell you what," Robin said, "we'll divide it up. You lot can keep one half and I'll give the rest to the widow and her children. If she hadn't given me a job on this boat we'd never have found our prize."

"Wait a bit," the skipper said. "That's not fair. If the widow hadn't given you a job you would never have sailed with us. And if you hadn't sailed with us we'd be dead men by now, or in prison. You won this prize all by yourself. You keep the lot."

Robin thought about it.

"That's true," he said. "I'll tell you what. You take the ship and sell it for whatever you can get. I'll have the treasure. I will give half to the widow and her children, and keep the rest. Then I'll give it to the poor. Those pirates robbed the rich. It's only fair if the poor get the money they stole."

"You sound like Robin Hood," the skipper said. "Robbing the rich and giving to the poor. That's what Robin Hood does."

"How do you know about Robin Hood?" Robin said.

"Everyone knows about Robin Hood," the skipper said. "He's famous from one side of England to the other. I'd like to shake his hand."

Robin thought about this on the way back to land. He sat on the deck of the pirate ship with the treasure all around him. He was choosing some earrings and a necklace for Maid Marian.

Shall I tell them the truth? he thought. *Shall I tell them that Honest Simon Wise is really Robin Hood? I think they'd like to know. The skipper wanted to shake my hand.*

Then he thought again.

Yes, everyone knows Robin Hood. He is famous from one side of the country to the other. He is famous for chasing deer. He is famous for shooting arrows. He is famous for robbing the rich and giving to the poor. He is not famous for being seasick. And the skipper has shaken the hand of Robin Hood even if he doesn't know it.

He decided to say nothing.

When the fishing boat reached land, everyone in the town was on the beach to watch. First the fishermen unloaded the fish.

Then they unloaded the pirate treasure. A great cheer went up from one end of the beach to the other as the men carried the sacks and chests ashore.

Robin went over to the widow who was waiting with her children.

"Madam," he said, "half of all this is yours. You took pity on Simon Wise when he was down on his luck. Now you will never be poor again."

"And what will you do?" the widow said. "You're a rich man, now."

"I shall give everything to the poor," Robin said. "I don't want to be rich. Rich men get robbed. I know all about that. And now I must go back to where I came from," he said. "My friends will be missing me."

He hoped that his friends were missing him.

Next morning he bought a horse and a donkey. He loaded his half of the treasure on to the donkey and rode the horse. Then he said goodbye to the widow and her children. He said goodbye to the fishermen and shook hands again with the skipper. Then he rode up the path to the top of the cliff.

The grey North Sea lay behind him, under heavy grey clouds. The salt sea wind blew down his collar. Ahead of him lay green fields, green grass, and the Greenwood.

He rode towards it and never looked
back.

Barrington Stoke would like to thank all its readers for commenting on the manuscript before publication and in particular:

Emma Austwick	Joseph Martin
Zoe Bennetts	Jade Pardoe
Kerri Bevan	Robyn Parker
Jodie Blakey	Olly Pascoe
Matt Burt	Amy Robinson
Laura Cox	Kirstie-Rose Gilbert
Jade Davies	Jamie Sanders
Daniel Firth	Kirsty Stringer
Oliver Griffin	Lewis Taylor
Sam Harvey	Nick Taylor
Laura Kirk	Sue Warner
Shaun Lovatt	Rachel Wilks
Mrs A Martin	

Become a Consultant!

Would you like to give us feedback on our titles before they are published? Contact us at the email address below – we'd love to hear from you!

info@barringtonstoke.co.uk
www.barringtonstoke.co.uk